www.FlowerpotPress.com
DJS-0912-0183
ISBN: 978-1-4867-1555-8
Made in China/Fabriqué en Chine

The Little Pink Rosebud

Sara Cone Bryant

Retold by Jennifer Shand   Illustrated by Sally Garland

This is the story of the little pink Rosebud.

The little pink Rosebud lived under the ground in her tiny, dark house.

One day, when all was quiet and still, the little pink Rosebud heard a tapping at the door. TAP, TAP, TAP, it carried on. It was quite noisy.

"Who is there?" she asked. "I like it quiet."

"It's the Rain, and I want to come in!"
said a soft, little voice.

"Well, you can't come in. I won't let you,"
the little pink Rosebud said.

But the Rain did not give up.
A while later, it started up again.
TAP, TAP, DRIP, DRIP on the windowpane.

"Who is there?" asked the little pink Rosebud. "Who is making that racket?"

The same soft, gloomy voice said, "It's the Rain, and I want to come in! Let me in!"

"No, I still won't let you in," she said. "I don't know you, and you make too much noise!"

Then it was quiet and still again. The little pink Rosebud was snug and silent, until there came a rustling and a whispering. RUSTLE, RUSTLE, WHISPER, WHISPER all around the window.

"Who is there now?" asked the little pink Rosebud.
"I am trying to rest."

"It's the Sun, and I want to come in," said a soft and cheery voice.

"No," she said. "You can't come in!" And it was still again.

It was not long until the little pink
Rosebud heard a sweet, little rustling
at the keyhole.

"Who is that?" asked the little pink Rosebud.
"Why do you keep coming to my door?"

"It's the Sun," said the cheery, little voice,
"and I want to come in. I want to come in!"

"No, no. I said you cannot come in and I meant it,"
said the little pink Rosebud. "Now please go away,
and take the Rain with you."

As the little pink Rosebud sat there all alone and trying to rest, she heard TAP, TAP, DRIP, DRIP, and she heard RUSTLE, RUSTLE, WHISPER, WHISPER. It was all around the window, at the door, and coming through the keyhole.

"WHO IS THERE?" asked the little
pink Rosebud. "I am getting quite upset!"

"It's the Rain and the Sun," said the Sun.
"It's the Sun and the Rain," said the Rain.
"And we want to come in! We want to come in!
We want to come in!" said their two little voices.

"Dear, dear," said the little pink Rosebud. "I am not going to
get any rest. This Rain and Sun are not going to leave me
alone, so I guess I will have to let them in."

So the little pink Rosebud opened the door and
in they came! The Sun grabbed her one little
hand and the Rain grabbed the other, and they
ran, ran, ran with her to the top of the ground!
Then they said, "Poke your head through!"

The little pink Rosebud poked her head through
and saw she was in the middle of a garden!
It was springtime and all of the flowers were
in bloom. They were beautiful!

The little pink Rosebud stood in the garden, and she was the happiest little pink Rosebud she had ever been.

• • • • • • • • • • • • • • • • •

Before a rose becomes a flower, it begins
as a tiny seed. That little seed is planted
in the ground where it is cool and dark. It
needs plenty of rain and lots of sunshine in
order to grow. Once it is ready, the seed will
sprout and begin to blossom into the beautiful
flower we see in the springtime. This amazing
process is called germination, and it is just
what the little pink Rosebud did in this story!

• • • • • • • • • • • • • • • • •